Top
Cat

Top Cat

SCRITC
SCRAT(

Lois Ehlert

Voyager Books
Harcourt, Inc.
San Diego   New York   London

O-KA-LEE
O-KA-LEE

I'm top cat.
Pet me, I'll purr.

I guard this place
in my coat of fur.

PURR
URR
PURR
URR

Boring job! Never see Nothing much happen in this dull house.

Who let you in?
One cat's
enough.

ME-OW
SCRATCH
SCRATCH
SCRATCH
ME-OW

SNIFF
SNIFF

I don't want to
share my stuff.

HMAN
CIET

SWISH
SWISH

SWISH
SWISH

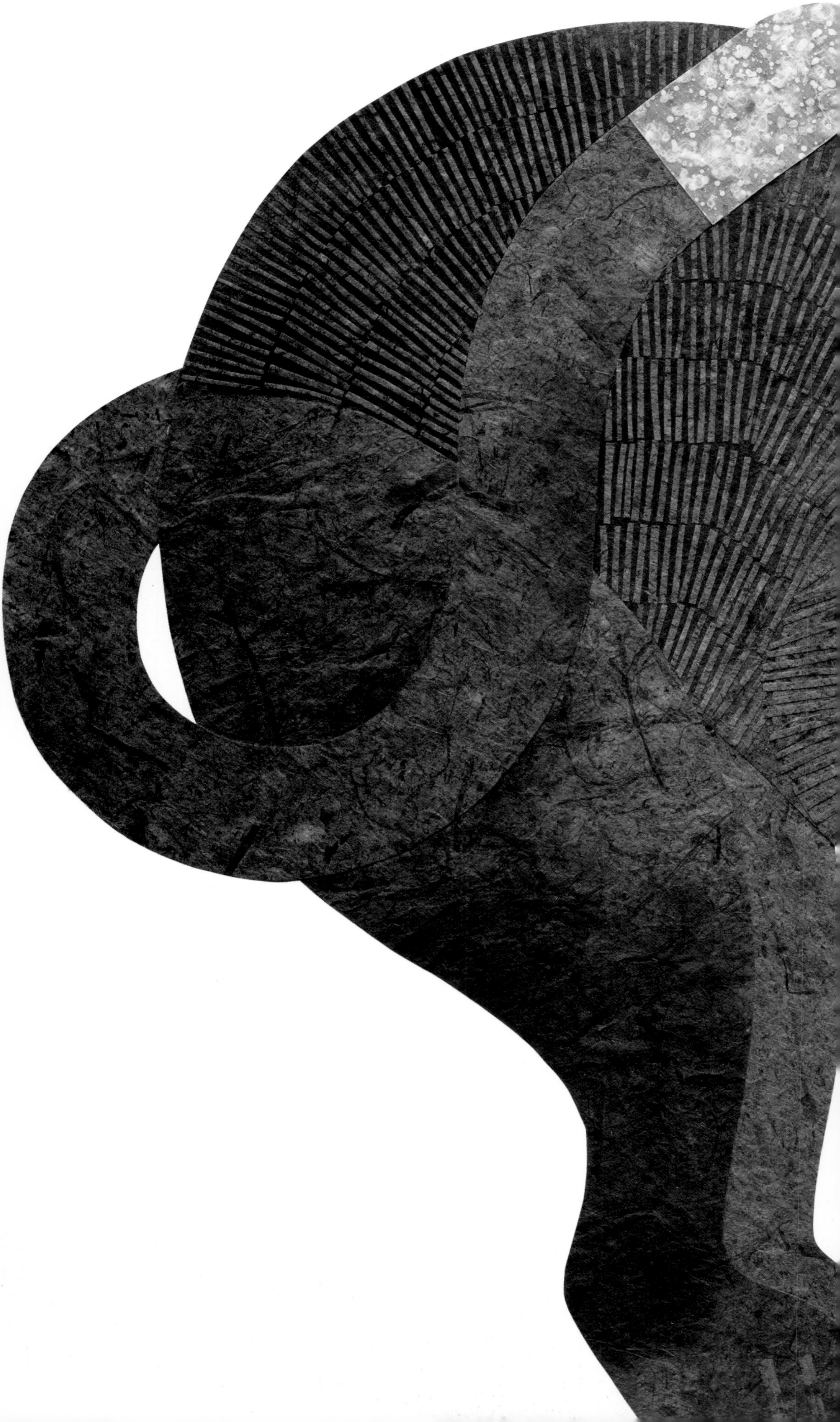

Go away, cat!

GRRRR
HISS
HISS

You've
invaded
my space.

SWISH
SWISH

CHEEP
CHEEP
CHEEP

GRRRR
HISS
HISS

And I don't like your cute little face.

SWISH
SWISH

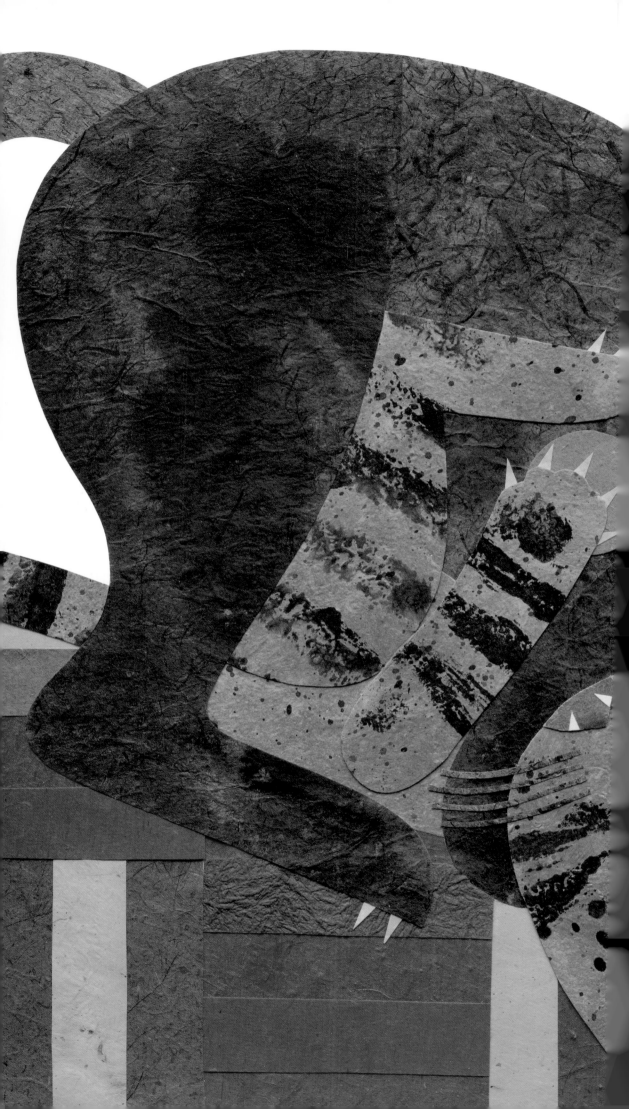

I'll fight you and bite
you behind the ear.
Get the message?
I'm boss
around here.

Well, you're here
to stay.
I can see that.

SCRATCH
SCRATCH

Guess I'm
stuck with you,
striped cat.

SWISH

JINGLE
JINGLE

THUNK

But
there's
more to do
than eat
and sleep.

JINGLE
JINGLE

WHIZ

Keep your green eyes open. Watch me leap!

Bounce on
the couch.
Leave
lots of
hair.

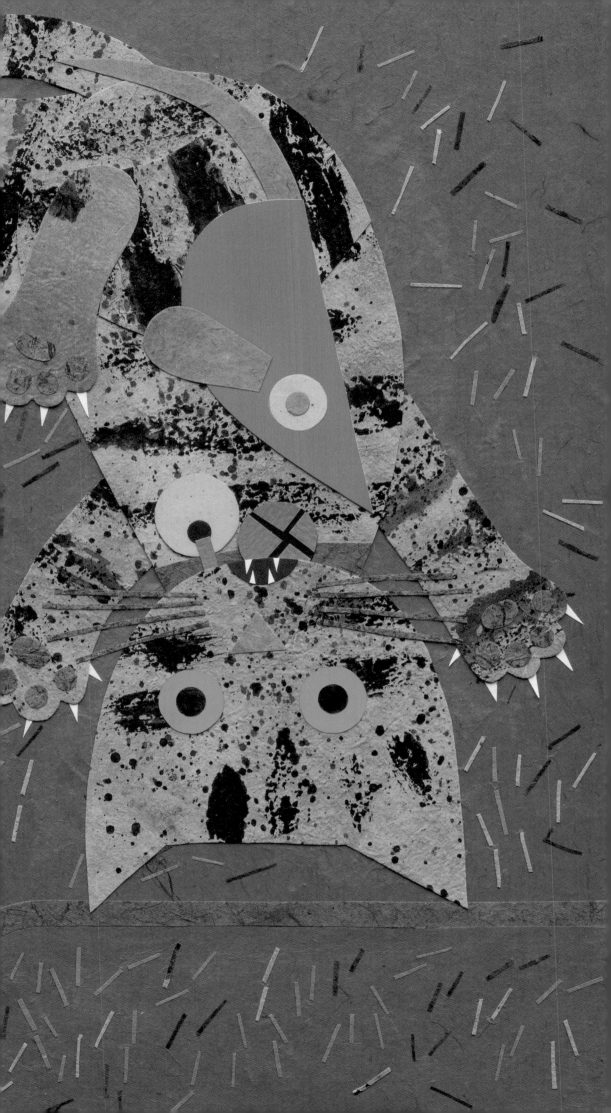

Eat leaves till the plants are bare.

CHOMP

Drink from the sink whe

DRIP

mpany's there.

TING
TING

JINGLE
JINGLE

BOI

SWISH

Dance on
the table
with the
silverware.

JINGLE
JINGLE

CLINK
CLANK

Door's
left open?
Go get
some
fresh air.

JINGLE
JINGLE

WHOOSH

Test your claws.
Give birds a good scare

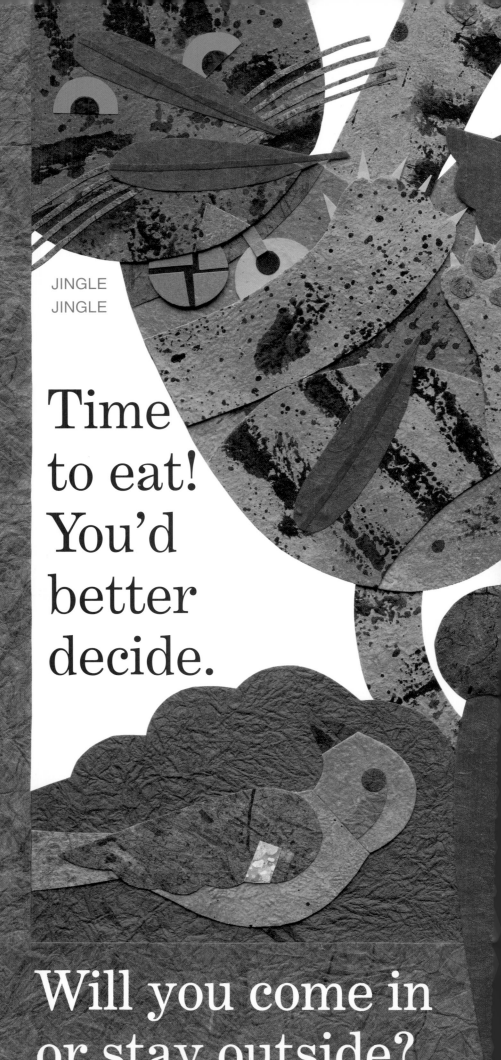

JINGLE
JINGLE

Time
to eat!
You'd
better
decide.

Will you come in
or stay outside?

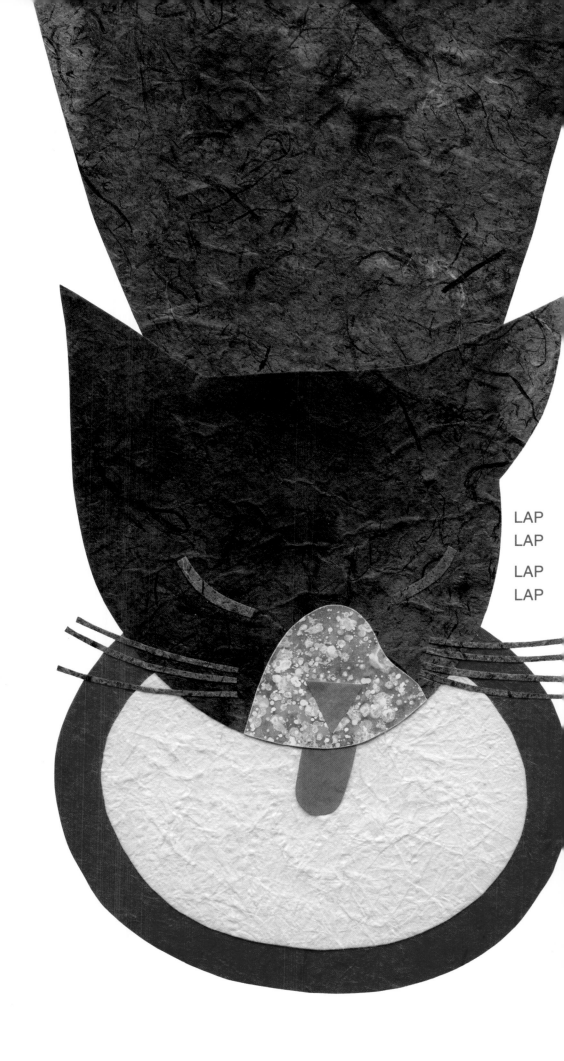

LAP
LAP
LAP
LAP

Welcome back!
Let's drink milk
in our furs.
No hisses,
no scratches,
no bites.

Just
purrs.

LIP
LIP
LIP
LIP

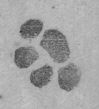

For Shirley and Don

www.harcourt.com

First Voyager Books edition 2001
Voyager Books is a trademark of Harcourt, Inc.,
registered in the United States of America and other
jurisdictions.

The Library of Congress has cataloged the hardcover
edition as follows:
Ehlert, Lois.
Top cat/Lois Ehlert [author and illustrator].
p. cm.
Summary: The top cat in a household is reluctant to accept
the arrival of a new kitten but decides to share various
survival secrets with it.
1. Cats—Juvenile fiction. [1. Cats—Fiction. 2. Stories in
rhyme.] I. Title.
PZ8.3.E29To 1998
[E]—dc21   97-8818
ISBN 0-15-201739-9
ISBN 0-15-202425-5 pb

H G F E D

Production supervision by Sandra Grebenar and Ginger Boyer